WHEN STORY STOPS, THE LEAK BEGINS

(SKAZ Music in 3 Acts)

When Story Stops, the Leak Begins

(SKAZ Music in 3 Acts)

John Sullivan

For information contact:
Unsolicited Press
Portland, Oregon
www.unsolicitedpress.com
orders@unsolicitedpress.com
619-354-8005

Cover Image: Jessica Sullivan
Cover Design: Kathryn Gerhardt
Editor: Caitlin James

ISBN: 978-1-950730-38-4

Don't tread on you? Entity. Of the Expansive Accumulative Society. Inalienable? Dyssynchronous! Siempre.

Rodrigo Toscano

To Tania Gutsche, Steve L'Italien and Aaron Green who helped me write this with their bodies, their presence and their collective will.

And for Jack Halstead, founder and first artistic director of Theater Degree Zero, who gave us all new eyes, and taught us how to use them.

TABLE OF CONTENTS

PLOT, CAST, AND CHARACTER NOTES

Plot / Action – A group of seekers tell stories, test their own and each other's limits, and establish boundaries on their quest for transcendent experience. Along the way they encounter allies, antagonists, grifters, back-stories, various strains of magic and are observed (maybe tracked, maybe served and protected) by an invisible entity living outside the story's mainframe. Think: *Canterbury Tales* meets *Hansel and Gretel* some decades into a *Bladerunner* future.

Characters –

Miz' Chan: A confident leader with a keen sense of justice; intelligent and mostly kind. But deeply wounded by the world, with a consequently cynical exterior and a very short fuse.

Mr. Rougarou: He can be somewhat secretive and introverted; his bayou lycan alter-ego is a "cross to bear" making real intimacy a "bridge too far." By hook or crook, or whatever else does the job, his "darkness got's to give."

The Right Reverend RSV: A true "sky-pilot," he taunts, cajoles, connives, conspires, conjures, and then holds out his hand for a "profundity requital." But he's plain about his motives, and he sometimes gives back more than he takes. In spite of himself.

Lady Striga: An ambiguous Two-Hearted being with Old World magic powers. It's hard to fully trust a

Two-Hearts but when she's hot, she's hot. When she's not, however, watch out!

aka "Doc Benway": He's co-opted the idea of *"Fail. Fail again. Fail better,"* and made it his personal spiritual practice. But mostly all of it without the better part. Is there any hope for this guy?

The Object-Monster (O-M): It's there but you can't see or feel it – unless you're Mr. Rougarou. And we're not sure how the sensory portrait of the Object-Monster really looks in the mind's eye of a lycanthrope. Every aspect of the O-M's being is a big, largely unanswerable question.

Who (aka The Big Who or The Big Bad Who) – The Uber-Being who dials all the dials, twiddles all the knobs, and pulls all the levers. The Ruler of Our World, *soi-disant.* Who knows all things (or so Who thinks) but we've never seen this Who, and this Who's not talking. We may need to ask Mr. Rougarou for some help with this Big Bad Who.

Some Notes on Hybrids, *Skaz* and Structure in "When Story Stops, the Leak Begins"

Like my own personal history, this text is a hybrid. The key component is the *poem-script*, a form that combines poetry (primarily dialogue), a performance script format, and a more or less omniscient fictional spy-eye lodged inside each character's head. These *poem-scripts* - considered collectively - though not necessarily in consecutive order - make a story by montage. A story with some urgency we are led to believe. Lady Striga goads aka "Doc Benway" to go fast, round up the children to "stop that leak and story the stone, once again." (Or else what?) Miz' Chan (and others) assert more than once: "when story stops, the leak begins." So you more or less have to assume that leak is not a good thing and the through-line needs to keep on keepin' on. The Slavic myth of Baba Yaga resonates with portions of the story and certain of the characters. The push for personal transcendence overarches everything. And then there's this (possibly) digital character unseen and unknown to all the others, but accurately sensed by Mr. Rougarou, the group's Cajun lycanthrope (aka *Loup Garou*).

The *poem-script* form of this story stems from years of making non-representational performances where speech conveyed content, but also led another life as a form of gestural action. You can find bits of Jerzy Grotowski, Eugenio Barba, Anne Bogart, and Joseph Chaikin scattered throughout the text – especially in the actions - but the prime movers are Juan Felipe Herrera (his *Noche Verde Nuclear*, in particular) and Rodrigo Toscano's *Collapsible Poetics Theater*. Influences from Commedia dell'arte, American Vaudeville, and even Mack Sennett's pre-talkie Keystone Cops add their own nuances to the mix. A series of routines or scat-patterns twine through the *poem-scripts* and work as armatures for opening and developing characters. The routines also impel the pulse, cadence, and physical rhythm of the text. These patterns synch with Lawrence Ferlinghetti's sense of performed routines and their meanings: "a song and dance, an experimental madness somewhere between conscious amnesia and involuntary megalomania," a sense of sharpening one's claws and thoughts through close engagement (or dialogic combat?).

So what about this *Skaz Music* thing?" Well, *Skaz* – or at least the idea of *skaz* as a characterization strategy - originated with Boris Eikhenbaum in the late teens of the 20th century, but I picked up on it from Joseph Brodsky's description of what he calls *skaz-yarning* in Andrei Platonov's novel, *The Foundation Pit*, Vasily Aksyonov's, *The Burn*, and the whole Russian *author-zong (avtorskaia pesnia)* movement – represented by Vladimir Vysotsky,

Bulat Okudzhava, Alexander Galich et al. For these artists, this prickly (or stoic or telegraphic or …) style of dialogue serves as an emblem of character and a key to each character's motivations, intentions, history, regional roots or even reliability as a narrator. Some more familiar examples of *skaz* in a non-Russian context include Kathy Acker's hybrid novel *Blood and Guts in High School*, William Burroughs's *Naked Lunch*, John Berryman's *77 Dream Songs*, and Eric Overmyer's play, *Native Speech*. Peter Greenaway's film, *Prospero's Books,* injects *skaz* into the editing rhythms and visual style - though the language is all Shakespeare. The dialogue in Guy Ritchie's *Snatch,* and *Lock, Stock and Two Smoking Barrels* is pure, unadulterated *skaz* – no matter how you feel about the overall quality of these films. And this is by no means an exhaustive list.

Imagine this text as a platform with plug-ins to accommodate readers, listeners, and performers. You can read these *poem-scripts* silently, scream them out loud "in full-voice" at the wall, frame the totality as a tricky, multi-voiced reading, or a more fully-staged reading that floats textual asides, exposition, questions, statements, and speculation thinly disguised as stage directions. Or just drop the static pretense altogether and you've got something strictly performative: like a live play for radio or podcast with an omniscient background voice to cut the cards and dole out glosses on the characters, concepts, and actions, as well as making live sound effects and laying down beats. A glossary of terms is included at the end of the last act to clear the air of questions, misconceptions, arguments or objections regarding meanings and uses of words, phrases and ideas. At least, that's the plan.

And that's all I can think of, though I've probably talked too much already. Like Eugenio Barba always says about the perpetual tension between writing and performance – and closely reading any text that's more than graphs and numbers is its very own species of performance – "only the action is alive, but only the words remain." Inhabiting our heads like ghostly "eye-lid movies."

ACT 1

"WHO"

"The heart, have you found the heart?
And realizing at once that none of them had found it,
they continued their way along the corridor, tapping
and listening to the mirrors."

The Miracle of the Rose
Jean Genet

(Establishing shot: Miz' Chan, Mr. Rougarou and the
Right Reverend RSV leap right into their fave routine:
"What's the Craic?" This kind of song and worry soft-
shoe is their inertial default whenever they're bored as
rocks, feeling froggy or in need of sharpening their
claws.)

Miz Chan:
So here's a teensy story about my mother,
stoned and transfigured

Mr. Rougarou:
So here's a truer story all about me-me-me:
on the day I was born
God was knocked out-loaded on the floor

Right Reverend RSV:
So here's a better story – ain't no lie, slick or shiny -
about my own mother
in the city where stone
statues walk & talk, and real people steady
transmogrify into stone-D statues ...
Bam! Just like that.

Mr. Rougarou:
So here's a cure,
But I won't ...

Right Reverend RSV:
... so don't.

Miz Chan:
So aim your body.

Right Reverend RSV:
So cut to the brains,
so–so–so–so

Miz Chan:
So true, so teensy, so very much better,
so shiny and so slick to boot:
when story stops, so sudden
our leak ... thus & so
it done begins ...

Miz' Chan's Hand Performs Darkness

**(Miz' Chan's hand performs *Darkness*
as she speaks.)**

Miz' Chan
Look: my hand
performs darkness.

**(Right Reverend RSV's hand performs *Everything* as
he speaks.)**

Right Reverend RSV
Lookee' here: my hand
performs everything …

Miz' Chan & Right Reverend RSV
… which is not my hand.

Mr. Rougarou
Wrong. Again.
You are wrong, again, you
are doing shine, not magic,
you are doing simple
"kick against the dread."
That's all it is.
That's what you really said.

Miz' Chan
Well!
Twist my teensy ankle
'round your neck

like a cuff.
Are you ghosting?
Again?

Right Reverend RSV
You feel that spooky leg against your cheek?
Like an oracle? Again?

Mr. Rougarou
No ghost, no leg, my own bitter mother
showed me (for-real and true)
a ceremony of hands:
bona fide like sky, like water, say, like sand.
Like the mud dream, too,
- she sure knew how to work that one -
like how in February
sky and water and you
will be this way
forever.

Miz' Chan
Forever ... tomorrow ... how's about now?
What say we interrogate that mud dream
right down to the core?
How's that rub your rhubarb, Baby?

Right Reverend RSV
Rub you raw, rub you all raggedy?
Spit out all that mummy-dust, little Baby.
Blaze & sleep!
Baby blaze! Again.

Mr. Rougarou
Full?
Or empty?
A Holy Ghost or just a *böser Geist*?
It's all ya'all's call, most very assuredly.
But even if you bury me upright,
a sweet spooky leg pressed close
against each cheek,
so, who's still laughing?
I got to keep asking that same hinky question:
blaze or flicker,
Who's still standing in the doorway?

Miz' Chan
(To Mr. Rougarou.)
Fie on full, as fie's on empty!
This highway's got more ghosts
and locks and ceremonies
than your own head's got rocks.

(Back at Right Reverend RSV, again,
with her hand as a challenge.)
This is real.
This hand never dies.

Right Reverend RSV
(Accepts the barb from Miz' Chan,
flings back the hand.)
This
is a real hand.
Betcha'!

Mr. Rougarou
Real, I suppose.
Real, but so very tiny.
Real. But just barely-merely there.
No pulse, no piper,
no trance, no sin-eater.
No charm against riving, wounding, or wiling.
Nothing that lurks or even transmogrifies.
Just another freak alert, real
in spite of being so, so tiny.
Every night-night,
like Hector's scary-bad dream of Achilles,
his brutal shiny teeth,
it's center stage, again.

Miz' Chan
(Tired of banter, feeling the urgency
to act, once again, Miz' Chan leans in
as Mage of the Moment.)
Like I said – Look!
My hand performs darkness!

(Miz' Chan's hand performs *Darkness*.)

I Sing the Body, Dysmorphic

(This routine is essential to stay the course of
civilization — at least the version Miz' Chan & the
Right Reverend RSV have imprinted on
and grown into.)

(Think: Tug o' War across a waste pit full of coal ash
floating in produced water
from countless fracking operations.)

(Think: "What I Haven't Got Yet Is Not From Want
of Willing, Trying, Killing, or Crying" vs. "Bet On
a Sure-Fire Winner
& You'll Never Lose.")

Body Image: Part 1
(Miz' Chan holds up mirror
and observes herself.
For Miz' Chan, she is, herself, a shock,
or a picture — or both.)

(Right Reverend RSV slides into his
Big Wonderful (but very Stupid) Shoes.)

Miz' Chan
(Reading the auspices in her mirror.)
Mirror, mirror …

(To Right Reverend RSV.)
This picture is *abgefuckt total.*
(Pause.)
Look. I might be a virus. I might be a ghost.
Look, I've got no teeth. Listen.
(Miz' Chan taps her teeth a few times, hard.)
I hate this picture.

Right Reverend RSV
(While he slides & skates and stomps around
in his Big Stupid Shoes.)
I never heard about it.
Don't know nothin' about it at all.
Know what I'm sayin'?
I, maybe, know that even though my piss is yellow,
my fine-feller's ass ain't even made out of gold.
But I sure do love these big beautiful shoes.

Miz' Chan
Listen.
(Miz' Chan taps her teeth again.)
I'm doing that thing with my mouth again.
(Big Blast from Miz' Chan.)
This picture is too much!

Right Reverend RSV
OK. You win.
It is a, hmmm, bogus, hmmm, worry routine.
It is a, hmmm, quirk of, hmmm,
organized yearning.
Don't you know that yet?
(Right Reverend RSV falls off
& out of his shoes.)

Damn! My damn shoes fell off!

Miz' Chan
You should get some better shoes.
(Pause.)
That's not what I mean.

Right Reverend RSV
Hey, I love these shoes like a sleepy infidel
loves his own furry turtle.
My red tongue says it,
long and loud
and hot-so too:
moon bless dreck
and wrack and rhunk ...
and these here shoes.
**(Pause. Looks way down,
perched on his Big Stupid Shoes.)**
See? Whew!
I can look way down from these here shoes.
(Pause.)
What do you mean?

**(Mr. Rougarou runs a *furry chew toy* up
& down his arms, legs, chest, etc.)**

Mr. Rougarou
Stay still, you Fuck!
Do it!

Miz' Chan
**(To Mr. Rougarou. Miz' Chan and grabs the
furry chew toy as she speaks:)**

Been doing too much zoom again.
Hah! You just zoom and zoom too much.
(1/2 Pause.)
Now you got to jitter, and jitter, and ...
jitter some more.
**(Miz' Chan rubs *furry chew toy*
over Mr. Rougarou's eyes.)**
Right here. In the hyperspace
of your own new eyes

**(Miz' Chan drops *furry chew toy*
in Mr. Rougarou's lap.)**

Mr. Rougarou
Open up body!
Welcome to the world of stiff.

<u>BODY DAMAGE: PART 2</u>

(A peek inside the World of Stiff.)

Miz' Chan
(To Right Reverend RSV:)
I mean: I'm doing that thing with my mouth again.
**(Miz' Chan demos doing that thing
with her mouth again.)**
That.
That thing I do with my mouth.
I hate that thing.

Right Reverend RSV
Lookee, Mommy, I'm cleaning my room.

(Pause. Right Reverend RSV doesn't
like this picture either.)
Jesus-Peezus!
(Now, mutter-mutter on the downlow:)
Forget this jerk. Heat up.
"Enact a goddamn force" ... something like that.
(To Miz' Chan)
Tell you what: this pain you scope
is, quintessentially, not my ride.
I stroll around & stroll around
in these here transcendental shoes.
All day long, I love these shoes!

Miz' Chan
Whew!
And what root have you been smoking?
Can't you see?
You've got some really stupid shoes.
And I got me an unpleasant mouth.
"No naked, sonorous, streaming."   Uh-Uh.
Just the Law. *Otra vez*, just that same Law, again.
It's part of this planet I carry on my shoulders.

Mr. Rougarou
(To his *furry chew toy*:)
Sometimes, it's real dark.
You see what I'm saying?
And then ...
and then you try to say: Pure No.
Pure No.
You see what I'm saying?

(Pause: while Mr. Rougarou
breathes like a sick engine.
He picks up the thread & ploughs ahead:)
Tell you what: I'm sick of this TV Monkey shit.
It keeps on. It adds up.
It goes both ways at once.
You see what I'm saying?

Miz' Chan
(Giving both Color & Commentary:)
So. Now the puppet's got no legs.
Again. Zoo-Buddha? Coo?
Get that itty-bitty swollen heap back
inside the lane of slow down.
This No. Not-this-No. Not-not-this-No.
I mean: Pure No? For really?

Right Reverend RSV
(Like an off-speed slider thrown
in no one's actual direction.)
Not no theory of vanishing invisible
clean contraire. Neither.
(To Miz' Chan, in particular:)
Whilst' you just ghost along, I glide my new world
alibis in these signifying shoes.

Miz' Chan
(To Right Reverend RSV –
a truly intimate extortion.)
Well!
Look whose mouth is Now:
A-sure-enough - Whew! – TEKNIK event!
(And now to Mr. Rougarou.)

And what's all this "Pure No?" Huh?
Like that's really gonna' happen?
Best go *Tee-Hee-Hee* and sneer
down the real dread.
**(Pause. Miz' Chan looks at
her own mouth again.)**
So, why is my mouth still laughing?

Right Reverend RSV
'Cuz it's yours.
'Cuz it's smack on your face. Whew!
An ill venue, indeed, for squeak or scream.
**(Right Reverend RSV topples over, off,
and out of his big Stupid Shoes.)**
Christ! Shit! Howdy-do!
My damn shoes fell off.

**(Right Reverend RSV remounts his big stupid shoes but
with obvious resistance
from said shoes.)**

Miz' Chan
I just don't like what my mouth is doing.
**(Pause. To Right Reverend RSV –
like a miracle in reverse,
or accidental enlightenment:)**
And you ... you like it down there on the floor?
All alone? With your shoes?
(Pause.)
Those *stupid shoes!*
(Pause. Miz' Chan observes herself again.)
I just love my mouth wide-open.
Like a movie star.

(Miz' Chan opens her mouth wide open
and <u>arias</u> with no sound, just like a movie star.)

Right Reverend RSV
Yeah?
Well hide all the guns.
Hide all the whisky, too.
'Cuz-I-just-love-these-here-shoes.
**(Pause. Right Reverend RSV slides
& glides & dances some more.)**
Wouldn't trade these shoes
for a shimmer-shimmer
kinda' ... spectophilic valentine.
Yeah: big, wide, beautiful ...**(Pause)**... shoes.
(Right Reverend RSV topples over, yet again.)
Damn! Damn! Damn!
My damn shoes fell off!

Miz' Chan
**(Her mouth unlocks from her aria rictus; she says <u>first</u>
to Right Reverend RSV.)**
Looks like your big beautiful shoes
just "ain't got no bone."
(And <u>now</u> (and *tenderly?*) to Mr. Rougarou.)
And O-You-Do-Too-Make-It-Burn, you do.
Compin' on the outside with your leper's rattle,
flyin' zoom-zoom-zoom inside your own head
like a suicide-drone.
And alla' time riggin' on it like a trouper:
when your mind says open
up to it, then your head says
gone. Says choke. Says
every Sefirot go take flight, go

hooji-booji black wing
in the City of Loom & Smoke.

Mr. Rougarou
So tell me here's a cure ...
but I can't.

MR. ROUGAROU *APPRECIATES* THE LAW
OF FEET

(Miz' Chan & Right Reverend RSV play with Mr.
Rougarou like he's a toy, like a bug
ripe to poke at. They monitor, probe
& inspect him up & down.
They laugh right through him.
They think they got him pinned.)

Miz' Chan
(To Mr. Rougarou. Like a jump rope chant.)
Run, run, you can't save nothin'!

Right Reverend RSV
Hey: it's a new law
just for YOU!

Miz' Chan
So unzip and stream.
So lockdown and pray.

Right Reverend RSV
Time to move it – move it
Rou-Body Blue,
Full of charm and fine velocity.
O-You-So-Are!

Miz' Chan
Brimming all strange and brittle.
Like the en-the-o-gen-ic splurge of stars
you know you gonna' be-come.

Mr. Rougarou
Yeah, yeah, yeah ...
I say it again, like I said it before:
On the day I was born,
outside the reach of this law, or that law,
God was knocked out on the floor.

**(Miz' Chan & the Right Reverend RSV tie plastic bags
on Mr. Rougarou's feet
as they talk to him.)**

Right Reverend RSV
Hah! Lookit' that there!
You got you some real nice feet.

Mr. Rougarou
Yeah, yeah, yeah ...
on the day I was born
God was too stoned and not so very beautiful.
Right there ... on the floor
– with my real nice feet! –

Miz' Chan
That's right
You got your very own feet.
Ungodly, or the other way, you got it made.
But now you got to make your own feet ...

Right Reverend RSV
... *appreciate* the Law ...

(What Mr. Rougarou does not appreciate is all this
nosey focus on his feet. Barbed, gnarly, claw-like,
positively lupine, his feet are a dead giveaway that
something's up with his own personal genome, and it
ain't that pretty. Based on prior close encounters with
livid burghers waving pitchforks and a slew of hairline
escapes, he knows he's got to think and talk fast here.
Even with Miz' Chan and the Right Reverend RSV —
whose acceptance or rejection of anyone seems arbitrary,
random, like they just jumped out from behind a bush
to go: Boo! — he can't parade his otherness.   And he's
not really sure whether they already know or not.
(So what does that mean?)
But he's convinced they could never
understand or feel his scene.
So sad it is, and Mr. Rougarou daubs
back a sad giant tear.)

Mr. Rougarou
Yeah! Yeah! Yeah!
You got the LAW part, but I, too, got the crawl
as much as I got my own feet on my own.
So what number do I call?
Whose mug do I dissemble?
Do I cop a common okey-doke?
Do I commandeer a cutie?
For fake or for temporary or headin'
for a fall? Tremble it more?
Tremble it harder? Tremble like
a phobic fear of sleep?
Or resurrect some fine and rigorous behavior
in the bathtub?
What's the dig, say?

What's the protocol?
I plan my mystery before I dive down deep.

Right Reverend RSV
No mystery, no plan implied, no protocol,
no phobic fear, no fake.

Miz' Chan
Gnaw your own conundrum 'til it's bone enough,
you *skaz*-talkin' porch-dog.
You sad alpha-stooge.

Right Reverend RSV
Where's your formal orbit, anyway?
Where's your anti-matter surge.

Mr. Rougarou
Orbit's sinking, falling, dipping.
Surge gyred down to a drip-drip-drip.

Miz' Chan
So's it's back to the Zone of Slink for you.

Right Reverend RSV
So's it's back to that ol' Avenue of Meat & Shake.

Miz' Chan & Right Reverend RSV
And always the more you want it,
the slower the train.

Mr. Rougarou
Woo-Wee!
Flesh-O-God!

White fields bloomin' in my brain, again.

Miz' Chan
'Til You is You, again,
it's Bye-Bye, Baby.
Back in utero, you go!

Right Reverend RSV
Baby, Bye-Bye. O Blubber!

Miz' Chan & Right Reverend RSV
O Foo, enough!

DON'T YOU DRAW YOUR DEVIL ON MY WALL

(A "pure" routine: High Noon in beautiful downtown
Burbank.)

(Miz' Chan & the Right Reverend RSV stand next to
their chairs & face each other. Sometimes, the Right
Reverend RSV almost takes off, then hesitates, then
doesn't take off his coat because he isn't wearing one.
Sometimes, the Right Reverend removes coat after coat
because he's wearing 3 or 4, or even more. Mr.
Rougarou sits in front of them like a tightly coiled and
morbidly confused spring.)

(They may say these lines as many or as few times as
they choose in the moment. They riff on harmonic
implications and throw each other "pick & roll-ish"
fakes. But, sometimes, they are entirely
straightforward about their intentions.)

Miz' Chan
What are you doin', Bud?

Right Reverend RSV
Takin' off my coat, Pal.

Miz' Chan
What are you doin' … Bud?

Right Reverend RSV
Takin' off my coat … Pal.

(Miz' Chan & Right Reverend RSV now sit. They do
a few *"SQUEEZE-AH routines"* from their chairs.
Right Reverend RSV does the SQUEEZE part.   Miz'
Chan does the AH part.
It's all in call & response style.)

(Mr. Rougarou also does *SQUEEZE-AH's* in a
shadow call & response pattern mirroring
Miz' Chan's & the Right Reverend
RSV's routine.)

(Miz' Chan & Right Reverend RSV stand up & creep
toward Mr. Rougarou both doing SQUEEZE-AHs as
if brandishing a weapon. Finally, the Right Reverend
RSV actually squeezes Mr. Rougarou. Then Miz'
Chan echoes with an AH. Repeat 2X, more or less.
Mr. Rougarou comes to his "senses" & stops them.)

Mr. Rougarou
This?
Not this?
Not-not this?
Not-not-not this?
Not?
What?

Right Reverend RSV
This!
All this, but of course!
Miles and miles and miles of nothing ... but all this.
(Pause.)
But you gotta know first ...

you gotta Ask ... Nice.

Miz' Chan
That's right, you know.
That's all this is.
This-this-this!
And more of This.
OK?
So ... Ask, now ...

Mr. Rougarou
ASK!!!

Miz' Chan & Right Reverend RSV
(A wake you up direct from
the legendary *Oleo Strut*:)
We thought you'd never ASK!

(Miz' Chan & Right Reverend RSV apply *Skinned-*
***Wolf Mask & Furry Arm / Leg-to-Foot Wraps* to**
Mr. Rougarou's arms/legs.
Say what? Again? But he lets them do it; we must
guess that this was what he asked for. While they
work on Mr. Rougarou, aka "Doc Benway" bursts
into song. Think: Son House without a link to Jesus.)

aka "Doc Benway"
(Sings: *"Don't You Draw*
***Your Devil On My Wall."*)**
Bang a nail down
Bang a body up to heaven
Bang a shotgun
Like a pretty baby-doll

Feed shotgun like a baby
And a baby grow up tall
Just don't you draw your devil on my wall

**(Between each verse: Foot Percussion,
Body English, Chain Drag
all across the boards.)**

Know my feet drag my body
Through the furnace
Feel the heat on my skin
As I crawl
Play with teeth, play with fire
Play a shiny rubber ball
Just don't you draw your devil on my wall

Got to scream, got to worry
Got to go and make the show
Goin' crazy by the phone
For a call
Got no laughin' bone above
Got no sky-juice sly an' all

**(aka "Doc Benway" twists last line
into a wicked holler:)**

Just don't you draw your devil on my wall.

**(Right Reverend RSV uncorks one last way-eerie
SQUEEZE. Mr. Rougarou squeezes himself, himself.
Miz' Chan arias the AH response.)**

(Mr. Rougarou bugs out on his SQUEEZE-AH phase
and shakes and twerks and shivers like an insane larva.
Like he's hot to lose the *Skinned Wolf Mask and
Furry Arm & Leg-to-Foot Wraps* wound around his
body by Miz' Chan and the Right Reverend RSV.
While he shimmy-shimmies, aka "Doc Benway"
comps on his blues kazoo. Miz' Chan & the Right
Reverend RSV frame the *mise-en-scène* with flashlights
on either side. In a blink, all at once, Mr. Rougarou
loses his momentum, slacks, shuffles, stops cold, and so
does aka "Doc Benway.")

Miz' Chan
AH-Um!
The Whenceness and the How
of the Shank Man's
stagger down.

Right Reverend RSV
So, when story stops,
the leak / begins ...

Miz' Chan
(At /:)
Hey, I heard that!
It's up to only me-me-me to say that!
You just stepped right in it, Mister!

Right Reverend RSV
Say, I don't see your marker
on this end of the genome.
Nowhere. No how. No way, Sister!

Miz' Chan
Well, maybe so, Baby,
but I can't see no symmetry
behind your old eyelid movies, either:
Tune in, some time, and take a peek.
That's where your own leak, begins.

(Mr. Rougarou, mask and furry wraps askew, stands
slumped over. Like a dead battery, perhaps, but still
he's thinking: "Leak? Leak?
What the fuck hath I/we wrought here?"
Miz' Chan and the Right Reverend RSV scan his
perfect movelessness with greedy eyes
and their flashlights.)

(While the others scan him and sleuth for clues, Mr.
Rougarou hurls himself psychically through time and
space for a little diegetic eavesdropping further on into
the text. To where Lady Striga winds up aka "Doc
Benway" with Spirit-Memory magic — if, in fact,
that's what she's doing. But wait! There's someone
(or something) else inhabiting this space. He can feel,
maybe even smell some(one?): smooth, digital,
hydraulic, maybe, ephemeral; some(thing?): cycling on
and off in a soothing hum, scanning him back,
affirming their contact, maybe? Another order of
being like unto himself, more or less?)

(This is a moment for Mr. Rougarou to remember, and
he does.)

ACT 2

"WHAT"

"… memory is an ally of oblivion …
a fish-net with a very small catch."

Joseph Brodsky (In a Room and a Half)

Miz' Chan Can Dance, but a Red Steel Vulture Don't

Mr. Rougarou
(Like a torch song with old school enhancements
à la Ella Fitzgerald and, maybe, Jack Spicer.
Maybe Mr. Rougarou has a bad case
of the Crazy Jane's for Miz' Chan.
So why are we always the last to know?)

Yellow horns go crazy
when a harsh lip touch 'em,
and Chan can dance
in a window, not no
secret to my eyeball in
a gold light afternoon, upon
so many hooves of commerce
cross a stone river, stone
backwards, each ghost
goes belly-up, goes
panic, goes show, and
show some leg,
like Chan can in a
window: soft fingers
of platinum draw
her outside on a red
light afternoon, palms
open, on her skin a
light, and gold, no
stone again, no
cosmologist groupie
in a "Cure" drag got's to

prune yet another patient, no
way, no one misses hats
more than the occasions
for hats ...

**(Mr. Rougarou breaks into radical scat
arpeggios & mimes, then aborts,
his own healing breakthrough.
Seamlessly, he returns to the tune.)**

...but a statue, *Herr
Wesen*, a statue of a vulture
is not-no-vulture, no
more than ain't no sense
in a long mile shine,
straight into actual
blue light afternoon, say
Mr. Red Steel Vulture got's
no future, neither, he
don't blink like
a vulture blinks, don't
dance neither like
Chan in a window
can breeze a note away
and still, and always,
ol' Red Vulture got's
to grook-a-long a fat mayor's
playpen, say don't droop,
Mr. RSV, make a drip-steel-drip
of red juice nether down
to snow, instead, nether
down in red muddles under

so sore hoofers slogging
by in a poor ol' sad ghost
bunch, and they can't
blink back, neither, can't
dance on a gold light
afternoon in a window
like Chan can

Lady Striga & aka "Doc Benway" Do Spirit-Memory Magic & the Object-Monster "Explodes"

(aka "Doc Benway" stomp-dances under the stars. As
dancers go, he's up there, all alone, on his own
gimcrack pedestal. Lady Striga hovers, draped
"like a sofa between tenants.")

(This dance is not for her benefit.)

(The Object-Monster also hovers somewhere in the
space, just below the wavelength requirements of
human perception. But this "cloaking" should not be
framed as an attempt at stealth or espionage. The
Object-Monster merely lives in a separate, parallel
dimension. Very objectively, of course! Independent of
the Big Bad Who, or so we can only hope.)

aka "Doc Benway"
I feel like a new
Stretchman Beast
at the bottom of
Goddess Secretes

I feel like a seismic rodeo,
that skin between us all:
I want it all back, now, I do
I want it all forever, now, I do, I do

And I walk it all, forever,
like a devil's orphan walks,

without sin and rolling-rolling,
- across oceans and oceans of serotonin -
And O what a good Phosphene
Cascade Commando, am I!

And I'll sell you fake supernal, unknowing, forever,
and I'll sell you my spectral, my only bastard buzz,
and I'll sell you starry maps
to run alive through the wire
to dodge all the traps,
to defile the temple fire
and I'll sell you the whole volatile-molotov-tensile-
manifest /

**(Lady Striga breaks into & enters aka "Doc Benway's
song at /. She shakes her drape with a loud crack &
aka "Doc Benway" freezes in place. Lady Striga
looms over him like a "Mother Manta.")**

Lady Striga
Hey, you old Dreamer-Boy-Baby, you.

aka "Doc Benway"
I know ...

Lady Striga
Yes. You do.

aka "Doc Benway"
I know that Voice ...

Lady Striga
I know you know that.

I know you really do.
I got no eyes, maybe, but at least that's real.
And my Voice means real trouble for you.

**(Lady Striga casts her drape over aka "Doc Benway"
like a net. She hums and "installs" pictures, symbols,
sounds-shards of "other people's core to die for," and
eyes, lots of eyes — all over the drape like EKG electro-
probes, or dermal time-release drug-pumps. In between
her humming, she unveils her bricolage / elective
affinity theory of memory for aka "Doc Benway's"
future use while he performs his "mission".)**

**(Think: Goody Rigby and her
Feather-Topped golem without any links
to Nathaniel Hawthorne.)**

Memory's a made up thing.
That's what we're steady doing.
You can dig away at memory, full-bore,
like a pit of gold, or copper,
or yellowcake: that tick, tick, ticks.
You can jig that memory, too, like an itch, and the
itch warms up, the warm spreads out, and that old pit
gets wider, deeper: it all goes tick, tick, tick.
Like a clock it makes you dreamy, yes it does,
makes you dream in all four directions, all at once.
Like you walked, fell, jumped, ran
right out of your history into something else
you, maybe, really need to see. Like an extra
chromosome, or secret gene, guards its dire
consequence: like deep pain
in a ghost limb you never earned but,

still, must wrap your skin around.
Like "ceaseless, inexhaustible" cold war, forever –
many faces, many voices trapped
inside the mire of their separate fates, the histories of
their separate clans – is, now, the organizing principle.
So now you can watch yourself with many pairs of
eyes: watch you watching you watching you ...then it
goes all raw around you.
Then it aches, maybe, like a crushed butterfly aches:
in your very hand that crushed it, now,
stigmata bloom. But, still,
you got to jig-jag that itch.
Soon enough, you still outrun your story.

**(Lady Striga finishes engineering her Feathertop. She
begins a chant to wake all the dead who look like
they're merely sleeping. She also imbeds a command to
move the action into a possible future. So who you
workin' this one for, Lady Striga?)**

"Nothing left but "Do It" for an old scratchy-man
Crawlin' like a beetle through wind-blown sand
Skinny bones a-buggin' like a hoo-doo tree
Draggin' back a bacon for baby and me."

"So go get-get-get all the kiddoes.
Round up them sonny-boys
and that moon-ish girly-O
"with a dark turn of mind."

"Wake you up, clang you heels,
run you hard, away."

(aka "Doc Benway" dreams himself
back into being. He "comes to"
in fight or flight confusion.)

aka "Doc Benway"
... this blood, new blood ...
- *Jehoshaphat!* -
these memories, new memories!
-        *Vergangenheitsbewältigung!* —
Like my skin's all crusty with 'em.
Their past, my past, all stuck together, now,
Ick and ruin, ick and ruin, nothing but
ick and ruin, here!
And all so very crusty!

Lady Striga
So Dreamer-Boy, you.
Look outside, look far away long, now:
What do you see?

aka "Doc Benway"
I see ...
I see ... bum and ice and dread.
I see ... Where-God-Does-Not-Live.
I see ... nothing happening, nothing much going on.
Will I be what I see, forever?

Lady Striga
So Blue-Dreamer. Yes, you.
Look inside, now, look teensy:
so what do you see?

aka "Doc Benway"
I see ...
I see ... gunshots, lightning ... fire, more fire ...
... I see, maybe ... memories,
forgeries of memories...
... bad checks, blown warrants, beat-boxers,
gun-gangs at the border...
I see "the wire's behind us both, now,
but our feet have turned to wire."

Lady Striga
Now you got yourself a real quest, you washed-up
ghost, you a true Zanni; now, you got you a duty,
now, a gen-u-ine mission. My own mission so it goes
is bringing this all through, just for you.
And yours is: just go fast, just go faster,
however long it takes: tell 'em
it's time to stop that leak and story the stone,
once again, once again.
Flesh or wire, flash or fire:
same need's still the engine.

(Now the Object-Monster senses another presence: not
Lady Striga or aka "Doc Benway," but some(one or
thing) almost invisible, appearing in the O-M's field of
perception like a dream in flight on furry wings. OK,
so we're anthropomorphizing like your typical dumbass
human supremacist here – but - cut us some slack,
please. It's just our temporary heuristic – we've got
nothing else to go on. To the Object-Monster these
beings are all others but this new (invisible?) other is
not like the other others in its own otherness. So what
will the O-M do? Well probably, wait prudently, of

course, for closer reconnaissance and bigger data to
prime more nuanced analytics. That's the default — just
like all these other routines we've seen unfolding — and
the O-M is good
with the concept and process of waiting.
The O-M never seems to run out of time.)

(Meanwhile, aka "Doc Benway" wanders like a dazed
bug around in a wobbly circle. Beyond these odd
arpeggios of gesture and emotion,
can he ever wander again with a purpose?)

aka "Doc Benway"
So where does this leave me?
So what, now, should I do?
Don't want to be a lost man, that's true enough.
Half-way out of my time into someone's somewhere's
else: just ain't no good no how
for me, or you.

(The Object-Monster, sensing a possible paradigm shift
in aka "Doc Benway's" core ontology, quietly
"explodes" rather than risk capture and the possibility
of humiliation or even disassembly.)
(Or so we've been led to think.)

Lady Striga
(Draped again — she does it to herself —
but speaking her own version:
a voice with hot-arc, a voice behind-beyond the pale of
standard protocols.)
You're buggin', baby, always buggin'.
You remember yet? You got to go and do.

Ain't but a few of us left, now, see.
When the bug bites you, no matter where you be,
you're bit, you're bit into: you got to go and do.

Bye-Bye No Fly Zone or Fugue for Miz' Chan

(Miz' Chan spins the cylinders of her .357 like a stunt artist. Miz Chan drags the Right Reverend RSV Center-Stage, flips him prone, pins him down with her knees & this is where it goes from there:)

Miz' Chan
Me and Nina Scalapina swirl & spin all night: La-la-la-la-la / (With slur & honk in tenor register) Buff Akropolis! / & every body's doin' UP / a rave / UP / every suture / every Faerie Grin / every hard anatomical accoutrement / totally suspect / totally beyond the ken of scope or probe / of nanograms / of thick wit / so, so we twirl & spin & twirl until dys-funk-channel baby 2 years in geometry when I was / like / all stink and hyper / (you know: ventriculatin' at de' ZaZu Pitts *Memoria* High School – like the gone & gorgeous *Zeitschatten* I always wanna' become), like / Whoa!! **(Big gulp-gulp of breath.)** / like I must remember to breathe / to breathe, like, inside the motion / like, remember to:

(Big Breath Out: sigh of the melancholic pain balloon.)
WOOO-WEEEE! /

& then dys-funk-channel / internationale / shooter baby wa-a-aves his conscious coma, wa-a-aves his / big / ass / cannon / awful-big-& lovely, too / his big / ass / cannon grabs my bop-top like a promise / & he laughs / through big, shiny, cinematic teeth / like

this: / **(Laughs: digital scream, hollowed-out bottom.)**
/ like he snides / *"so where is my baby-baby?"* / like
any question like that question deserves a bra-a-ave
story / and then he utters new dystempers: *"live meat
don't need this kind of stuff"* / & then, dys-funk-
channel shooter baby spits a love song through that
rack of shiny-big teeth / like shabby Technicolor, in
its sad decline / clampt' together in a sex-growl /
(Growl: the cat in the moon, gives it up like a dog.) /
he sings: *"each ghost, each ghost, each ghost nearly
finished"* / & then / & then & then he like pumps 10
rounds into the ballroom/ like hot, smokin' into
space, like / at the wall / or all the layers / of eyes /
or the space behind the wall / of eyes / like hot-hot,
you feel the burn go by your face, see? / like now: the
wall begins the wail begins to wake / like now: all
make shrines / pray / blubber in their cameras / so I
get up & Nina gets up / & we spin around & dance
until the cops come / this one cop tells us to stop: /
HEY! PARK! IT! / **(LAUGH: Pseudobulbar
Incongruent Jag.)** / like Nina stops / bites the floor,
hands locked behind her neck / but I don't stop, can't
stop / I-am-too-jacked-up-to-stop / & I twirl myself
around / & around / laugh-spin-laugh / **(LAUGH:
PIJ again.)** / & then & then … / like he makes me
stop / then he like grabs my arms / then he grabs and
holds my arms against me / *"You tease, I tase,"* says
he / holds my arms against me / then I stop / no fear
yet ... but / my blood gets all heavy / sinks down /
like / like octanes of stop / spread / sleep / like dead
forevers / like no more *fun-fun-fun on the Autobahn*
/ like / my blood changes back / to fear, mostly /

changes all the juice all the charge all the motion in
my blood back to fear /

**(Unsteady riff on Anguish, now, & then, Lamentation.
Then, another very short PIJ.)**

see? / only mostly / like when I got to move-move-
move / when I got to move / it's just not cool-cool-
cool / like jammed inside a sleepy coma, the Mama /
like her babies / like the photos of her deep blues /
face down in the rain / strewn across the lungs of a
cold sea / on the bone edge of *"Don't worry. / Your
babies are always, already embalmed."* / born to be /
like that / on the stone edge of Un-Coil / Un-
Mother / on the scary edge: Un-seeing it all / forever
/ where charge & juice & motion go / not cool, not
ever / keep, it / hard / hazed over / think-it-do /
freeze & sleep / like that / wrap the Mama in a
shroud ...

**(Miz' Chan spins the cylinders, again, like a stunt
artist. She empties each cylinder: rounds hit the floor
(reverb of echo); runs barrel of the .357 down Right
Reverend RSV's bare, sexy back: light, empty &
throw-away pro forma as a social kiss, unyielding,
occasionally tried but only, provisionally, true.
Ultimately, her mouth winks back at her, her motions
lack commitment. Miz' Chan, too, makes a soul
shrine. But she's too cool to just say it. So don't get all
smug on us, Miz' Chan, or drop your guard. Still and
yet, you and me and all of us, are just another bunch of
little Who's, on the prowl or on the lam. And while
the Big Who truly hallows such sacrificial discipline,**

such butoh-like restraint, the Big Bad Who "don't
never / just give away / no reprieves.")

... so ... her babies move / move-move-move /
against haze / inside freeze / room to room,
unmoored / her babies move-move / lids open /
unmoored / from memory / by heat & muscle /
move & go & drift / by burnt synapse: ashes, ashes /
go way away / every dendrite: jiggy on its own pyre /
in this world / in this world: wither on the brink /
Mama sad, the Mama / in this world / Elektra glides
into mourning.

Little Baby Bunting's Gonna' Go a'Hunting

(As Miz' Chan drops the .357 & walks away from the
recent crime scene, the Right Reverend RSV gathers up
the gat, the unspent shells she ejected and reloads while
he sings a "sing-song(y)" rhyme for kiddoes
in "less than vegetarian" times.)

Right Reverend RSV
Little Baby Bunting's gonna' go a' hunting.

(The Right Reverend RSV moves through a potentially
hostile time-space with stealth and caution like special
ops police do: sighting up one side, then down the
other, then up toward the ceiling, then down at the
floor with his huge gat. Sometimes he twirls to face a
possible assailant behind him; he obviously enjoys
making these moves. He's (also) obviously seen these
moves in a number of Action-Thriller movies. Think:
Charlize Theron tracks a Willem Dafoe-Christopher
Walken hybrid (or maybe just another failed done of
the Big Bad Who) with fake ice / synth-venom in her
eyes through a labyrinthine terrorist —
or corporate, or both - command center.)

Little Baby Bunting's gonna' go a'hunting.
(Pause.)
Hey little baby, c'mon out from where you're at.
It's time to swallow up the whole moon
in one big gulp.

**(The Right Reverend RSV runs into aka "Doc
Benway" and focuses his weapon
on this possible perp.)**

"Hey! Ho! Let's Go!":
"I got you in the sights of my big gun."

**aka "Doc Benway"
(In a disgusting display
of groveling servility
and calculated ass-saving:)**
Hey, I don't do flim-flam; I don't do lurk no more.
I sold my serge extortion drag
to score me a pardon.
So are you here to kill me, or to spare me?
My head is whole, but now my legs,
in fact, won't work.
Look at me: my life is no bargain - paid off in full,
with all the perks still intact –
but I'm still on your side, I am, I am.
I couldn't run to save my own hide,
even if you dare me to.
I'm hung, Daddy, take me away.
Are you here to kill me, or to spare me?

**Right Reverend RSV
(Lowers his gat.)**
So. OK.
I can't because I won't because I don't have to.
(Pause.)
So. OK.
You win!

Aka "Doc Benway"
How Much?

Right Reverend RSV
O-so-very-much-of-it!

(The Right Reverend RSV tosses aka "Doc Benway"
the .357, throws up his hands & inches slowly
backward and away.)

(aka "Doc Benway" cradles, then spins the gat – like
a rusty stunt-artist. He twirls around and faces Mr.
Rougarou – who's been standing there, motionless and
(possibly) invisible to the others, all along. Perhaps
Mr. Rougarou is sniffing out the Object-Monster.
(Hey, is the O-M down here, too?) Mr. Rougarou's
lupine pedigree from way far south and down the bayou
lets him smell, see, and hear many beings and
phenomena below the perceptual radar of all the others.
We'll dwell on that ourselves a little bit later, if we get
a cue from the Big Bad Who.)

Aka "Doc Benway"
So what d'ya say,
gets to thinking:
you like to play?
Well I play, too, say
you become what you play.
What you say, you become.

Mr. Rougarou
Me? Play?
No play, *no se*, down here, does

63

no good to pray, down here's not
the story of a true star.
(Pause.)
Get-off-me.

Aka "Doc Benway"
So what d'ya say,
get's to thinking: you're
either full of spit, full
of venom, or never born,
period, right?

Mr. Rougarou
Full or empty? That to me's
a false dichotomy, to-be-sure.
Why not just bury me and get it done with?
There's no cure, and who's laughing now, huh?
(Pause.)
Get-off-me.

aka "Doc Benway"
**(Points the gat more purposefully at Mr. Rougarou:
aka "Doc Benway" must convince Mr. Rougarou that
he's a seasoned assassin, and actually savors the deed.
Should Mr. Rougarou believe him? Do you?)**

Gets to thinking: tell you what, doin' this
dark number moves more gravity than all-else-
ever, if your mind cares to go there.
First, you feel like fallin' down sad:
"O what a waste, what did I do?"
But then, you feel bad, brutal too,
like a loud hot steel whine.

Then you feel proud, and fatal,
and primed to go again!

(aka "Doc Benway" tosses the .357 to Mr. Rougarou.
He catches it, examines its shape (and heft &
suchness?), weighs its meaning & significance like the
provincial outlier
from the *Pox Belli* that he really is.
And all the deadly props and traps that go with that
insanus terram.)

aka "Doc Benway"
(aka "Doc Benway" kneels before Mr. Rougarou, and
bares his chest in a positively pontifical gesture. Think:
Henry Fleming carries the Union oriflamme toward
Confederate ranks at Chancellorsville, hoping to taste
cold steel or hot lead and win his own *Red Badge* but,
yet, and still, it's all – just in his own head.
Aka "Doc Benway" guides Mr. Rougarou's gun-hand
so it's centered directly on his bare heart.)

There you go: it's one-on-one.
Mano a mano.
Una cabra loca por otra.
You. You. You
can drill this guy.
He had his chance, once,
but now he's yours, alone.

Mr. Rougarou
(Tosses .357 back to aka "Doc Benway.")
Get-off-me.

Aka "Doc Benway"

Listen up to me, son-son-sonny-boy,
looks like you aced your trial.
I'm talking straight, *fair dinkum*, now:
time will be
a new race will come on to us
out of these stars
while they're still close enough
to see us watching them,
our faces stitched up with sorrow.
Like saints, like sailors,
they'll be to all of us,
coming wrapped up in kindness,
a fresh new age of grace – power
of masters, science, jailors, industry,
abruptly snapped, reprieved, replaced
by something better than our worn-out tomorrow.
Better than this dark and faster
slide by inches into dying.
(Pause.)
There, I said it: now it's
your turn to believe it.
Say you swap your organs of abuse
for an open throat, a bigger lens,
"fac-tu-os-ity," buried in the bone.
Say you no more run through fire, stop
trying what never works no matter what.
Say you no more make your dire Mama grieve.
(Pause.)
And what say you?

Mr. Rougarou
Get-off-me!

An Ars Poetica for Mr. Rougarou

Part 1: This Is the Shot

Mr. Rougarou
(Juggling that ol' wave / particle
duality, yet again.)
Nothing is fixed. Go on, chew
my head, peel back my face, see
into I am not who I am, I am no accident,
neither / nor. This is my air, too, my teeth,
all my pretty shiny ones, my sex text,
my wet mouth embodies ... basically: I fuck-
it-all, or I fuck nothing, at all, embodies:
"Criminy, get-off-me," embodies: vectors,
verging, wolf whistles flung into space,
embodies: plasmic heft of matter,
embodies: fluke sparks of force
in parallel chatter between dark
and light sectors, embodies:
goes both ways at once ...

Part 2: However

Mr. Rougarou
(Like calculated havoc.)
Or next, go ahead and don't see: I
don't need eyes, I don't need
dark or light, sectors or streetlamps,
wave after wave ringing
in my brain, or tender aches,

particular to skin, and stuff.
No shoe, no feet, no-no-no "stain of love"
singing shrill, singing tough upon.
That leak in the sky, every time it kills you.
Every time, it kills you.
I don't need a body
that bonds you, then it binds you.
I don't need a body with brakes.

(Miz' Chan, Mr. Rougarou, and the Right Reverend
RSV move light and careful through something that
may be a deep forest. Right Reverend RSV serves as
"way-finder" for the group. Though not without some
justifiable grumbling in the ranks.)

Miz' Chan
(She growls:)
So where in this drag dog Ministry
of Sackcloth and Sour Mash / leavin's …

Mr. Rougarou
Or, of a day, this day and its very own cleaving: it's
Beguiling, bereaving and so, we go and
where in this Ministry of *Peregrinatio ad Coeli* …

Miz' Chan & Mr. Rougarou
(In unison:)
… are we goin' to?

Right Reverend RSV
Goddoggitt!
Your Growl-O sure is Tasty-O!
Though's I know not what you're speakin' of
you're goin' where you got to be.

(Right Reverend RSV gestures "hands way up to the
sky" for a credible vision, for magic transport,
for more animal presence.
Think whoosh of updraft.

Followed closely by a combination
flurry of thud & crash.)

So: lay all ya'all's eyes upon me
and behold: "The Navigator."
Crawled out from underneath
the Stone of Destiny, I did,
one dark midnight upon the Hill of Kings.
Left hand steady, fomenting strife and siege,
right hand swellin' up the peril all around this
fishbowl of an Anthropocene.
It's down to me, now, he who stride
around all fuzzy like a nut.
Like an iffy mushroom, see, see, with me: it's all
comin' up three's!
Just maybe?

Miz' Chan
Yeah, yeah, "Navigator," go rub your own growl
three times over like a genie.
I see nothing but that same sky. Again?

Mr. Rougarou
Same sky don't get it done, Daddy.

Right Reverend RSV
Daddy, indeed, O-indeedy-do.
I'm way up here in the pulpit
just for you, and you, jumpin' up and down,
transcendent: and, to boot, a little stoned on it.
I am the last best wild track west,
absolutely original

para-para-psychic
bone-print of the actual,
One thousand feet of fire
rushing to eat the neighbors,
(I'd say it's high time, now,
to high-tail it out of town).
Whew! Still jumpin' but it could be
could be, could be, too, something
Pomp and Beautiful to do.

Miz' Chan

To do … to do, you say?
I do my own do on my own.

Mr. Rougarou

I do my do with dignity, Dad.
Doin' it til I'm dead, I am.

Miz' Chan

A beast to boot.

Mr. Rougarou

A rap I cop to.
I take it while it shines,
Rosetta.

Miz' Chan

Hot and Meat-Hungry, I do, too.
I do likewise unto you,
You Hallelujah-Mongerer.

Mr. Rougarou

Me, too. Me, too.

That could be my very own do, you're doin', no?

Right Reverend RSV
Whine, whine: blue-biz-blue.
And I suppose and do you know
what to tickle, what to suck,
without me here to show you?
Hello, again, you're out of luck, and always.

Miz' Chan
O Brave New Happy Mouth!
You're killing me.
Show us some Brain Ranch
or set us free:

Miz' Chan & Mr. Rougarou
(in unison:)
Ignition … Lift-Off! Boom!!

Right Reverend RSV
Indeed, indeed, this zoom-zoom
ride will never full-belly be
for thee & thine, again.

Mr. Rougarou
O-Mr. Daddy, Mr. Daddy-O,
it's no payback we lack.
No guise on the outside, neither.
Die-Young-Stay-Pretty
don't get it done, Dad.
Show us some Skull.

Right Reverend RSV
OK, OK, Ye hollow Blurs of Bone.
We are here! We are here!
All ya'all Drop-Dead Blues Entities, we are
here where I fall, God-Struck, from my horse
and tell ya'all, precisely: Scope
the transubstantiation of growl into cower,
where one swell's fly angularity be made straight:
brimmed over, like I say, and like I like it:
Fully fuzzed, fully nutted, every orifice left ajar.
Call in all thy dark birds, now, from their
skulks in their corners and have a sit.
And let it all go down. We're here –
or, at least, you are:
time to adapt or just hallucinate for days.
This is your Jones talkin'
and none of my own.

Miz' Chan
Here? Here, you say? So here is where?

Right Reverend RSV
A place where you can't get to without me.
A place where I can't go.

Mr. Rougarou
Where? There? And where is what?
My dreams tell me they can live
longer without me,
grow legs, greedy hands, and fly.
My dreams tell me they may
someday kill their dreamer:

Bye-Bye, Baby. They say
it makes you stronger - but you still gonna' die.

Right Reverend RSV
It's simple, dreamers, simple as spit.
Parse it, goose it, yank out the death-
kit and twiddle some knobs.
Apply a little dire flux and fiddle and
how and soon, soon, you're one foot on the moon
and one foot in the fire.

**(Pause. Right Reverend RSV is glad to be almost done
with his role as *"judas-goat"*
and eager to just "disappear.")**

But now's I got to go back over to
where blood's the most thick,
where beasts, the most ferocious.
I got's to go and do my own do,
on my own.

Miz' Chan
Well go then, go.
And UR! to you. May you
never stop wishing you stayed
to do your do …

Mr. Rougarou
May peace, for you, remain always
just a rumor - and lame, and
further-evermore - for your ears, alone.

Right Reverend RSV

Careful what you're working, sister / brother,
I'm not a better angel, not even, I never
had a mother, and you know,
I left many warriors laid low,
aunties, kiddoes, saints that failed their finals,
All nailed to the devil's very doorway,
wrapped up in a pretty bow.

**(The Right Reverend RSV makes a secret-sacred sign
that best fits his current eschatological frame over
Miz' Chan & Mr. Rougarou as he says:)**

So I leave you *absolutio ad cautelam*.
Best I can do. Best to dream on, too.
And sheerly, enough for both of you.

**(Miz' Chan & Mr. Rougarou step over Lady Striga's
home turf perimeter. This activates her digital stream
of traps, lures, sensors, magnets, & leads them to her
virtual hidey-hole in the very heart of the forest. The
Right Reverend RSV - no longer with them, embodied
- is always near in spirit.)**

**(This also activates the Object-Monster - whom we all
thought (maybe) exploded in a prior act of heroism / or
maybe simple pain-avoidance. The Object-Monster
hovers over Miz' Chan & Mr. Rougarou - like a
"digital angel?" Something about them both seems
portentous, but the Object-Monster needs more data to
decide just what that something is, and why. Perhaps,
also, a (digital?) skeleton key to the human meaning of
portentous?)**

(Mr. Rougarou instantly goes hyper-vigilant when the
Object–Monster switches on: he sniffs, he senses
something, maybe due to his partially Cajun /
partially lupine corner of the genome.
He's been down this road before.)

(Miz' Chan & Mr. Rougarou enter their sleep-screens
and glide straight to Lady Striga. She's arranged herself
within a *de rigueur* shamanic expert tableau with a
huge book (of ancient arcane pedigree) in her lap. This
moment is borrowed from centuries of Faith, Doubt,
and Chicanery. Think: postmodern crone meets a
timeless, more pedagogically inclined
Baba Yaga with no sweet tooth
or urge for tender meat.)

Miz' Chan & Mr. Rougarou
(Their sleep screens flicker awake, but briefly. Miz'
Chan & Mr. Rougarou find themselves sitting cross-
legged on either side of Lady Striga. In unison:)
What? Who?

Miz' Chan
(Miz' Chan is a quick study.
She quickly schools Mr. Rougarou:)
No Fear. Don't scream. I think we found the beam
that pulls us: *Come Hither.*
Let's give this old bird half an ear, together.
(Miz' Chan & Mr. Rougarou resume
their digital fugue state.)

(The Right Reverend RSV barks an order from
somewhere outside the perimeter. His command
disturbs & (maybe) mystifies the Object-Monster who
still has a lot to learn about these beings.)

Right Reverend RSV
GO!

Lady Striga
Though everything I say or do is just a quote,
what I now read to you is not just
an ad for the real act.
No parallax, no tedious
Arguments of Perihelion, here.
It's all reconciled over miles of light years, see,
I can only feel what I can memorize and say:
from me straight into you, direct from
the source star, *O People of the Book*,
it's time to listen, and then to, maybe, pray:

***Lady Striga Sings an Ancient Fable
of All the Old Men, Sleeping, Raging, Roaring,
& All the Old Women, in Full Glow***

Old men rage in sullen bathrooms, listen:
How they choke, throats full of gall and goddamn,
Their boots kick hard against the goad, again,
Again, they're kickin' it, and again, *how it doth ram.*

Old men rage in fallen hallways, kick up a roar,
Full of broken teeth, empty windows,
All bare to thread,

Listen: how their pang & throb rocks
The secret wounds of a gone world open,
Shakes down a new world they can't
Even name, holds a next world, always,
Like a pale flame in its palm.

Old men rage and lurch and buck
And fall down under willow trees,
Old men slam shut heavy-lidded orbs
Of eyeless, pointless, flicker, and freeze:
And so they are just what they be: old men,
Old men, all of them, together, doze
Away the century.

Old women walk, all light-foot, together, carry
Lamps and astrolabes that glow,
Forever, up and down bare hills,
Past pine woods lake, down to the beach
On ghost-patrol, and winding,
Winding, always winding
Beyond reach, and nervous, like a snake.

Old women float with stars in their hair, faces
Flecked with ice, hard weather on their brows, Hard
weather in their gray-green
Snow leopard eyes: one foot in this world,
One foot in some other, hands
Driving hard the great dream of Heaven.
Always right, they've never
Got a reason; always ready,
Their paradise is now.

(Miz' Chan interrupts the digital trance.
Mr. Rougarou is just a scooch slower to ignite.)

Miz' Chan
Bloody Hell!
You've all lived in vain.
Your God's gonna' cut you down!

Mr. Rougarou
**(Also interrupts. His speech is more
like prophecy without anathema,
or unkind jive-ass slurs.)**
Caught in a fog of sighs,
Insane wind howls through it.
A whole crash-yard of flattened isms:
O what a fire for the future!

**(Lady Striga makes some sort of hand-to-screen swipe-
like gesture to reconfigure her digital palette. She
reasserts control over tone and timbre,
theme and tempo.
She speaks-reads again.)**

Lady Striga
Listen to The Book. All us *People of The Book*,
listen how the book speaks to all us people
in all possible ways at once.

(Lady Striga continues the ancient tale.)

"Where are you, old men," each old
Woman calls out, carrying a sense of doom
Soon to be on her back like a papoose?

"What are you looking for? Why does it matter?
Where's your little House of Nod
All tucked away, snug?
Where do you hide your ghost in the daylight?
Where do you lay yourself down to have
A say, a sit, a sigh, a sing, even, maybe?
Where do you lay yourself down to disappear, Now
that the dream lock's sprung open?"

"Back in here, old women, where light don't
Reach, the I, the we, speaking for
The tribe," says one old man, then another,
Voices all wired up in a fist.
"Back in here, I/we feel changes; only feel,
See, I/we can't give the change a name
That's proper. I/we think we're
Growing souls, now.
I/we know we'll never fly, or fight
Again, or kiss no more. No more.
It's gone. It's over.
I/we showed us something, showed us more,
Showed us nothing much at all."

"Burn the church, I/we say, now: do it.
Don't care which goes where.
Have it done. Have it done. Have it done."

Blue Light-Red Shift: comes on in waves.
In full, never two of them quite the same.
Old women feel the pull of stars, the
Gravities of weather, they turn and lift
And hover over all the old men, declaim

Like thunder:

"Good night, good night, old men.
Sleep you boldly.
Shout us in your dreams."

(The Object-Monster (maybe) fears for Miz' Chan &
Mr. Rougarou. S(h)e / It jams Lady Striga's network
& "the two" come to.)

(Lady Striga softly flagellates her head, then dons her
official Helmet of Sad-Pointless Memories. Miz' Chan
& Mr. Rougarou throw barbs her way as they flee.)

Miz' Chan
Arch, eldritch, dire: one sick what-cha-ma-call-it'.
But now: time to bounce!
This stream of rage & roar & shiny-shiny ladies,
brought to cure or brought to rot,
becomes less & less curious-_er_
as on & on & on it goes.

(Mr. Rougarou sniffs the air before he speaks.
Can he smell – almost see – the Object-Monster with
his Cajun-lupine gifts? Or maybe
just its ghost-print?)

Mr. Rougarou
(To Lady Striga:)
So the wet-shroud, footless, goeth a'ghosting?
This dirge you do works my nerves like a drug.
And this dope-sick drug is a doomer.

(Miz' Chan & Mr. Rougarou step beyond Lady
Striga's perimeter. They shake off the traps, lures &
sensors and prowl the "forest," again,
free-thinking monads that they are.)

(The Object–Monster closes her/his/its "eyes."
Could that expression be a smile?)

Lady Striga
It gets so dark so early now.
(To Miz' Chan & Mr. Rougarou:)
Remember me: a made thing.
A frayed-around–the-edges, smudged, and grayed-
out, sun-bleached thing.
A laid-down burden, prayed over thing.
Remember: remember-some-thing.
(Now this aside slices through
her heart like a scalpel.)
This next time, I want a better daughter.
This next time, she's the big one
and he's her long shadow.

(Pause & Regret? – not a mood you normally associate
with your typical shaman. Generally speaking, as a
sanctioned cartel of psychic professionals, they just
don't look back.,)

All this air around is so damn big
and I am so damn little.
Jesus … I cry so easy now.

(Lady Striga freezes: one sad giant tear emblazoned on
her cheek.)

Right Reverend RSV
(From his secret point-of-vantage
just outside the perimeter.)
"Journey agents" of pre-history: cast off
your chains and you best remember
how "the rich ones go to bed
with good whiskey in their heads."
Only that. Only that.
Remember the whip of history.

(The Object-Monster lifts an "eyelid?"
Something like disquiet, here?)

ACT 3

"WHY"

Bakunin: *Left to themselves, people are noble, generous, uncorrupted; they'd create a completely new kind of society if only people weren't so blind, stupid and selfish.*

Herzen: *Is that the same people or different people?*

Tom Stoppard (from **Salvage** *- part 3 of* **The Coast of Utopia***)*

(aka "Doc Benway" lays in a heap.
He wears his slouch hat & eponymous cheap
sunglasses, with walking (magic) stick nearby. So is a
large, empty, foul-smelling jug.)

(Miz' Chan, Mr. Rougarou & the Right Reverend
RSV stumble upon this phenomenon: a misplaced,
disheveled, possibly comatose aka "Doc Benway."
They collect data, assess the scene, deliberate,
occasionally poking at aka "Doc Benway's" earthly
remains like an abandoned vehicle.)

Mr. Rougarou
Ecstatic seizures of grief and disappointment?

Right Reverend RSV
(With toe-poke.)
Ectoplasmic murmurs of bereavement
and over-ripe nostalgia?

Miz' Chan
**(A whiff off the empty jug
knocks her clean a'back.)**
Canned heat or just embalming fluid?
Either way a lot less ecstasy, a lot
more infamy, or fear.
The ghosts of other sounds, music, voices,
like – listen all around –
like Chaos calls the tune for Cosmos here.

(aka "Doc Benway" pops up into a full sit. Mr.
Rougarou and the Right Reverend RSV prop him up to
speak. Think: Marat in his bathtub before the lights go
out for good. Miz' Chan leans closer
to aka "Doc Benway's" face.
Think: Charlotte Corday,
l'ange de l'assassinat.
It's July 13ᵗʰ 1793: once again, a thick-dark
sense of pervasive menace is palpable.)

(So where's that infamous shiv, Miz' Chan?)

aka "Doc Benway"
This I that I embody-in-life
was dreamed up by my enemies.
Sure as shootin'.

Miz' Chan
Ah Misery Gee! You'll always be
feathers and bones to me.

aka "Doc Benway"
Some ghosts want to drag us
into their world by the hair.
But I'm already well-haunted.

Mr. Rougarou
If you're really a product of chance and
just making do, can you tell me
the last time a ghost was wrong?

Aka "Doc Benway"
Dead leaves in my pockets … damn this dark stain!

Ghosts creep into ordinary chit-chat
like the residue of a dream … like,
listen to this one.

**(aka "Doc Benway" begins to talk-out
the Brobdingnagian dream-haunting
that shook loose his very core.)**

*aka "Doc Benway's" Origin-Song of the First Blue-
Scream*

I found a blue baby
Fallen down from the sky,
From a spider hole in a war zone
Washed up on the beach

A baby just as big as
A big old single shoe,
No bigger, light as air,
Blue, and still, alone,

So's the surf snatched up this
Little blue baby, tossed it back
Into the water, like a bone, you know, but it
Could have been my unknown

Daughter, lost son, my
Seed, an early version
Of me – phy-lo-ge-ne-tic-ally –
Bleeding back from yonder, or another

Future to be, a parallel track,
It could have been all
The music in the world
Yet to come

**(The Right Reverend RSV, Miz' Chan and Mr.
Rougarou interrupt to interrogate the nasty first
premise behind aka "Doc Benway's" dream. Like:
"let's suppose this baby was mute, not inclined to
music, or just so many strains
of random proteins,
all jumbled up together in a sloppy knot.
Would that make this blue baby's being moot?
Or not? Or what?)**

Right Reverend RSV
Wow-Zaa, Sport! Where did you get that wound?

Miz' Chan
That little blue baby was a being, real enough!
Not an It. Not just a skein of gene-stuff.
You didn't try hard enough.
Now's the time to cry, hard enough and long.

aka "Doc Benway"
Hey, that's my being you're bouncing
back and forth like a "shiny rubber ball."

Miz' Chan
His being he says, and
why does he be at all?

Mr. Rougarou

Why does he be so much
without even meaning to?

Right Reverend RSV
He bit the "Big Be," once upon a time,
and then the "Big Be" bit him back.

Miz' Chan
Now he's preternaturally
scared: of not being at all.

Mr. Rougarou
Like the Big Bad Who's gonna'
snatch him up, give him a good-hard
nudge, and make him free-fall
into some massive, silent, hungry void.

Right Reverend RSV
Blank and bare.
That's it. That's all.

aka "Doc Benway"
Been all the way to being
and back again to not.
Here, listen to me,
it's a total immersion: we are all orphans.
Everyone can't just die
and become more than a doomed arrested version.

**(aka Doc Benway" resumes his blue-scream dream-
talking:)**

So's I cast my net way out in the water
To catch up the little baby -
Cold, blue, bare, wan – maybe empty like my
Own eye - but my net couldn't hold

The baby, forever, no, not even: It's all
Written down, somewhere: bloody dazzle, screaming,
atrocities – old ones and newer - but my net
couldn't hold the baby … the baby …
And the cold-blue baby was gone …

**(Done with his dream-talk, aka "Doc Benway"
probably expects some sympathy or, at the very least,
an uncomfortable silence.
That's not to be the case, however.)**

Mr. Rougarou
Your selfish genes, your hollow music,
You ought to be ashamed.
You need your own day of ire
with that lost blue baby.

Miz' Chan
Like try disremembering your own self,
for a change. Like loss, pain, the crush-stream story of
what is / what might be hence
just wriggled out -*de novo* –
from behind your eyes
like teensy little worms.

Right Reverend RSV
Before the neuron cascades commence
to crackle and fade, before the inevitable

jump-cut to dopamine drip: Do It!

Miz' Chan
Love is selfish, too, and
greedy, anytime it's starved.
Hang on, *viejo*: there's a savage
unraveling ahead for you.

Right Reverend RSV
And here is where "the wicked catch afraid."

aka "Doc Benway"
And here is also where my own
skull sings back to me:
the story of beginnings that crawled
inside my ears and, just, died there?

**(Miz' Chan, Mr. Rougarou and the Right Reverend
RSV mosey along to somewhere else leaving aka "Doc
Benway" alone, face-to-face with the import of both
his dream and his / their reaction to it. So, of course,
he bursts into song, as if we wouldn't notice
the lack of closure.)**

*aka "Doc Benway's" Prelude to The Gloomy, Self-
Absorbed, "Worried Ol' Hard Disease" Blues*

Got this worried ol' hard disease,
Got me walled up in a desert cave,
Got me collared, booked, and locked down
In a black box on the bottom of the sea
O save me do
O do save me

So's I fell down to pray, so
At the first break of day, so
And these Furies with a warrant
And a writ to kill
Snuck up on me
Snuck up on me
And stole my spirit clean away, so

(aka "Doc Benway" enjoys a preposterously public
private moment savoring his bogus-brazen (& silly-
primitive) indication of something he (maybe) feels is
deep and fully earned, or even logically warranted.
Think: a thin wind barely strokes the skin of an
opaque, muddy, mostly stagnant pond full of algae &
bacteria, tires & the occasional stolen car. A quick take
on this impression (just for the rest of us), & aka "Doc
Benway" exits pursued by the world, the flesh
and the devil.)

(& all the Big Who's devil's devils, too.)

ON HIS WAY TO DAMASCUS AKA "DOC
BENWAY" HITS A BIG BR(I)CK WALL

(Temporarily abandoning his shambolic career
disrespecting the life-force and dodging any bolts of
self-awareness aimed in his own direction, aka "Doc
Benway" resolves to drop the act & turn himself
inside-out to see if there's really anything in there. As
far as protocols or formulas for such a project, aka
"Doc Benway" employs a multi-cultural (or neo-
Colonial-appropriative, depending on your POV)
strategy of bricolage to kludge together a compass and a
viable way-of-working these psychic interiors.)

Miz' Chan
(Speaks directly to aka "Doc Benway.")
Ghosts (or gods) are not at war with beauty, or life,
or rain and gale-winds, or even the oppression
of so many brains tuned to vibrate, all at once.
They are at war with *You.*

Right Reverend RSV
(Narrates the ritual, antidotes the poison:
aka "Doc Benway" (and the others)
respond in kind.)

Ecce homo, **and his own personal "Rip, Rig &
Panic":** how this weak and delusional raggedy-man
chucks off his baby-skin, strips down to his own fat
shadow and sings his wilderness to fight for his life,
and atone for dismissing or freezing out
both the almost living and the nearly dead.

See the *Brood* awakening: how his hubris offends and
infuriates all the gods and ghosts - they're always right
on top of us, and every hidden realm projects its own
goblins like shadows across a heart. *Topu, Aos Sí,
Duppy, Jumbies, Xapiripe*, etc., mobilize in a blink to
ensure their covert dominion's immunity from
potential human stain. Eventually, he's struck down
for his defiance by *ghost-sickness*, blurring space and
longing, and left "weak with fright."

Watch him lock: how he stiffens,
young people carry his rigid body on their shoulders
around in a "widening gyre."
They smile while they carry him for his body shines -
this fever of remembering transfigures most – and his
luck, or lack of it, rubs off.
They say: his story outruns his life.

(Miz' Chan, Mr. Rougarou, and the Right Reverend
RSV stop gyring and set aka "Doc Benway" down –
actually straight up, standing still, stiff as a board.
Gradually he loosens up, wiggles his fingers, stretches
the rest of his body. The *Brood* disperses like Oberon's
gang of anarcho-syndicalist faeries,
dissolving into Max Reinhardt's iris,
in a quick shrink to gone.)

Mr. Rougarou
Look: his lips move …

Aka "Doc Benway"
O-My-O-My, now that there's the cookies.

Cross my heart and hope to stake my very being:
I just cut right through the blur.
I been strictly out there on my own
for days, you know.
**(aka "Doc Benway" throws his own self
on the "mercy of the court.")**
AH! So very much: AH!
So very much hard-used Heaven.
For Beauty's sake alone I stand convicted,
my own star in my mouth,
deaf eyes perched up top my spine
like twee standing stones.
O Happy Brain, flash and fervid,
into the Mother of Heavens unfurled, again.

*(After the Brood evaporates, the Object-Monster is left
to ponder (through enhanced multivariate analysis,
presumably) the what's, why's, and how's of aka "Doc
Benway's" recent ascent from the ranks of those "who
died as men before their bodies died" into a more
rarified community of the duly apologized and more or
less shriven, waiting on their next assignment.)*

*(At least that's a possibility, though the Object-
Monster plays her/his/its cards close to the vest and we
have no way of knowing the parameters of any
"thought process" involved. Another idea: it's possible
aka "Doc Benway" actually saw, was touched by or in
some other sense contacted the Object-Monster when
the Brood blew through his body. Maybe he thought
the O-M was just another form of astral punisher, like
the Topu, or one of the Aos Sí.*

*The O–M's obvious recon mission notwithstanding, is
the Object–Monster here to answer
any of our questions, or primarily
to challenge our theories by beaming back and
(possibly) distorting the realities they were designed to
reflect in a cognitive ricochet effect?)*

TRANSFIGURATION, & IT'S INEVITABLE BLOWBACK

"Rise up, right now, everywhere,
all of you: seize the whip of history.
Reclaim your common sky."

Vladimir Ilyich Ulyanov (Apocryphal)

(The original iconic version of the above directive was allegedly (issued-declaimed-decreed-unveiled?) as Comrade Ulyanov stood defiantly (or so we are led to believe), planted on the hood of a commandeered armored car. The moment was later captured as a stone sculpture - officially commissioned through a Byzantine sanctioning process by apparatchiks in the Artists Union of the former USSR. Since the late 1920's, this simulacrum of Comrade U chopped out of solid rock has remained (maybe still does, somewhere?) stolidly immobile - at Finlyandsky Vokzal / the Finland Station in St. Petersburg (site of the Ur-event, itself, on April 16, 1917). His stone mouth gaped (still gapes?) wide, frozen in a stone snarl; his stone hands were (are?) raised in a Socialist-Realist mudra that indicates: "exhorting the masses." ... O Ozymandias ... O common sky, forsaken.)

(aka "Doc Benway" lies prostrate.
He wears a black blindfold across his eyes. His old-school slouch hat, big magic stick, and eponymous cheap sunglasses lay near him. He could be dead, but probably not. He could be sleeping, or knocked-out

loaded, but again, probably not. We think he's
marshalling his juices for a last run at something
significant: maybe magic, maybe more so.)

(Lady Striga watches from above.
She will have no real skin in the unfolding action.
She doesn't know that yet.)

(Miz' Chan, Right Reverend RSV,
and Mr. Rougarou stare at each other.
Eventually, they touch with single fingertips
& shed their eyes of suspicion.
Miz' Chan cues finger-tip-touch
with barely audible: "Do It.")

(Miz' Chan, Right Reverend RSV
& Mr. Rougarou flap-snap identical red blindfolds:
they flap like damaged birds, they wave them to one
side, then the other, then overhead, etc. Close to unison
(but not quite). They wrap the blindfolds around their
heads, covering their eyes. Miz' Chan cues the wrap,
saying: "Do It." Louder, more forcefully than before.
They lie down, stretch out
prostrate: as in Holy Orders.)

(aka "Doc Benway" rises up
like a drunk swallow. He circles the others: makes
contact with his fingers, smooths hair, touches feet &
hands. He stops & stares (apparently) through his
blindfold at his own hands. Then aka "Doc Benway"
picks up his big magic stick & conducts himself:)

aka "Doc Benway":
I was told, already.
I accuse myself,
Myself
(Pause.)
I was told to smile inside the motion,
I was told to go pick a bone and unclench
- big fat fool of a chance on that one –
I was told: "You ain't been miraclized, yet,
I was told: "Not yet, You ain't allowed to drop."

**(Low wail of wind & elementals:
Lady Striga riffs with it. Maybe she believes she's the
uber-conductor. Maybe this gives her sufficient leverage
to unleash her "rich inner life." Lady Striga will
ultimately disabuse herself of every illusion but
motion.)**

**(aka "Doc Benway" defaults to stock routine.
Think: something that lurks between
Bert Lahr & Bill Irwin. Or possibly,
Spalding Gray in a more peripatetic incarnation.
That magic "schtick" he wields
really comes in handy.)**

aka "Doc Benway"
I was told: ain't no all left
ain't no all left, ain't
no, ain't no all left
but

I was told, and syn-chro-nous-ly,
that we all still want it all

100

but

ain't no all left I was told
and we all still want it all, alla'
time, and we all still want it all, alla' time, we do
and

tell you what I learned, I
learned: to sweat, to see and sweat, to see
a ghost, to see and sweat a ghost into keen be-ing

Be-Stir
Be-Stir

say ghost inside say shine say skin, all original,
say sprung a leak, it happens but it ain't no excuse:
to see, to sweat, to strain,
to give good crawl
again …

**(Hollow, slow hand drumbeat
adds to low wind wail.
More inspiration-delusional
energy for Lady Striga?)**

one time: it's a Grail
you got, then a cough, then a flower, then
a black bone, maybe, then a bomb ticks inside …

**(aka "Doc Benway" rocks the aria.
He dedicates this moment to Robert Johnson.)**

… then Paradise? Now? Hah!

Again? Hah! Hah!
Maybe? Truly? Present tense?
Hah! Hah! Hah!
And sense?
And "dust my broom."

(aka "Doc Benway" tries to dust away
the scars, sorrows, and distortions of his memory. His
recent brush with the *Aos Sí, Xapiripe,* and possibly
the Object-Monster left him feeling (simultaneously)
vulnerable but, maybe also, a tad immortal.)

Tell you what: an eye sees in a future
what an eye sees in a memory.

(aka "Doc Benway" "boxes the compass" with his big
magic stick to accommodate the full scope and range
"of this all.")

of this
of this
of this all

(aka "Doc Benway" laughs in spasms,
hurts himself & lurches back
to his starting place.)

I was told, already.
(Pause.)
I accuse myself.
Myself.

(aka "Doc Benway" addresses
his prostrate "children.")

Adios, Muchachas y muchachos!
We split – We split – We split
into shards of heat and "cold specks,"
into splintered bytes of corrupt memory.

(aka "Doc Benway" slides the stick over to the region
of the Right Reverend RSV.)

Catch ya' on the rebound, my Cuz-ez!
Don'tcha' know, it's all I can do.

(aka "Doc Benway" flops face-down, a purely
horizontal swan-dive, bellied out like a bed-sheet in
the wind. Then he hits the boards.
He stretches out prostrate —as in Holy Orders.
He comes to a dead stop.)

(Lady Striga finally cottons-on to her own irrelevance
in the course of this process. She leaps down off her
perch, puts one hand on her heart,
the other in the air above her head,
spins rapidly like a dreidel,
& yo-yo's off into the ocean.
Maybe to sift through the sand
for that cold blue baby?)

(Leaving us all with a
more or less ontological question:
Is a life without even the illusion
of agency any worse, or any better?)

(Miz' Chan, Right Reverend RSV,
& Mr. Rougarou – still blindfolded –
probe with arms, pointed fingers.)

(Begin *"thee raven zion"*: run 3 track audio mix (with
repetition as necessary) until Miz' Chan, Right
Reverend RSV, and Mr. Rougarou
work their graceless alchemy & are gone.)

(The three crawl closer together.
Their fingers touch.
They pull each other upright –
like folding up a tripod.)

(Right Reverend RSV finds the magic stick. Mr.
Rougarou carries Miz' Chan piggy-back. Miz' Chan's
arm stretches out to hold Right Reverend RSV's
shoulder. They move out as one pulse, one heart and
push against the impossible weight of promises,
sorrows, that whip of history we were told
not to forget.)

(Straining, sweating, and always un-seeing /
disremembering it all - & of course, the weight of those
promises and sorrows always pushes back, and the
whip of history stings and cuts –
they travel together:
literally and ideographically,
joined at the bone.)

(Their odds of success are pretty remote, their efforts,
totally unreasonable, but of course, that has nothing to
do with it. How GM Hopkins always says it:
"Dapple-dawn-drawn …
the achieve of; the mastery of the thing!"
That's the transluminal essence
of their form & their motion!)

(Abandoned and forsaken like a warped, cracked, and
misshapen old stone likeness of poor Comrade Ulyanov
cloaked with snow, nose buried in the cold-cold ground,
aka "Doc Benway" never moves, again. Just
figuratively, of course: you've got to see this from our
post-prandial, post-modernist, post-constructivist,
post-bop POV.)

*"Around that which is luminous within us,
there exists a shroud of darkness which we can
penetrate but cannot annihilate."*

Jerzy Grotowski (Towards a Poor Theater)

**(They've assembled their iconographic vehicle
for extended psychic travel. Now Miz' Chan,
the Right Reverend RSV & Mr. Rougarou move
together toward distant stars, the cold
darkness of space, amnesia, oblivion.
Or somewhere else.)**

Miz' Chan	Right Reverend RSV	Mr. Rougarou
	meanwhile,	
O-angel		
watch	back at the movie:	change
the "angel	tan town	
of the city"	tin bullet	forever
is	like we know?	crepuscular
thee	also	shine
raven	real	*por vida*
watch	almost, maybe	
is also	slow, fool	seeing
terror	sweat	
nervous		too much
to what extent	*corrida*	
dominion?		too often
O-angel	total	too deep
is also	translation	

thee
vengeance?
raven
throne
upon
who sits
there?
dreams
a format
for an angel
to be:
this dream's
next worry,
next mouth
opens into
blue flame
O-angel
is thee?
O-horror
is an angel?
of surge
nervous
raven
fist
of give it
up
thee-
O-angel
raven
stare
mouth open
wait
to breathe
O-angel
fears and

of terror
swimming through
"distant, great
and invisible"

practice
evasion:

choose -
a
history
to be, or
you can
perform it

busted
seed
no room
no need
for any
end
but
It

"O acknowledge
mine"
unexpected
true
as if lived before:
it

memory-
sickness:
this strain
of darkness
eaten
like air,
"diaphanized"
- these
rituals are
pure
poison

por vida

forward
forgetting
no va
knocked down
to rise
up
no va

life echoes
voice
echoes time
echoes
life
back
every
cycle
way short

cradles
nervous
vengeance
is zion
nervous?
is
zion
next?
to
come back?

to come
home?

I can't
live

here, either

next
communion
opens into

soft
rain

nexus
of
it
as lived before
spawns
a slew
of ghosts

a praxis
to worry
my eye

a child's eye
can't belie, can't
believe
it
either

here

"God's loneliness"

dead leaves
foot-
prints

run-run
outrun
my story

por vida

white nights,
where
no-no
December

shadow

walks

por vida

"stuck on

my eyes"

*"Never did I breathe with such a sense of
responsibility. I read a nobleman's soliloquy right into
the commissar's face – this is what I call life."*
Marina Tsvetaeva (Dark Elderberry Branch)

(So what, now, of the Object-Monster, lurking (but
not really) somewhere in the vicinity of Lady Striga's
(maybe) rash abdication, aka "Doc Benway's" utter
abjection, and the (possible?) collective ascension of
Miz' Chan, Mr. Rougarou, and the Right Reverend
RSV? S(h)e / it has seen (possibly felt and even
"empathized with") such a broad spectrum of human
feelings and actions, some of them clearly motivated,
some not so much. From *Vaudeville Posturing* to *High
Play*, from *Snake-Oil Huckster Spirituality* to *St.
John of the Cross*, from *Spring Awakening* to a gross
Anatomie of Abuses: so much mush and vanity
sharpening in the sun.)

(And what can all this mean to such a being? And
what would such a being do with the huge trove of
associations, suppositions, potential chains of causality
and arcane lore pent up in all these data? But there is
one thing we can probably count on: despite that ruse,
early on, the Object-Monster did not / will not
voluntarily explode, and seems genuinely intrigued – if
that's the right word – by the fate (or destinies?) of
Miz' Chan, Mr. Rougarou, and, maybe even, the
Right Reverend RSV.)

(Maybe the Object-Monster will continue to monitor
and eavesdrop, to record, to measure and graph their
progress toward wherever their ideographic mélange of
multiple wills leads them. After all, the Object-
Monster seems to be "on a mission" — or so its
demeanor might lead us to think - and after that
mission is completed, or even merely scrubbed for lack
of useful application, there needs to be an explanation
of methodology, raw (and cooked)
results, some discussion of implications
and recommendations for "next steps."
A final report card, as it were.)

(Or maybe, after all, the Object-Monster is a true
devotee of personal erasure, or a practitioner of
something like an extreme form of Bushido for whom
seppuku is the only honorable outcome for any failure.
We don't think so, but only time will tell. We don't
even know what constitutes success or failure for a being
like the Object-Monster. Or whether that Either-Or
algorithm has any relevance at all in the O-M's
cultural *weltanschauung*. Comrade Ulyanov may have
known all the answers to these questions — being such
an avid fan of immersive surveillance and using all that
amassed domestic intelligence data to leverage fellow
citizens in collective "Leaps Forward" or NEP's or in
implementing successive Five Year Plans - *mise en
abyme* - with a Zen-like non-attachment to results.)

(At any rate, it's now too late to ask him.
Or so we have been lead to assume.)

AKA "DOC BENWAY" SINGS A LITTLE LULLABY

aka "Doc Benway"
(Back-lit, like a shadow (or a ghost)
from his favorite hootchie movie.)

Then, night pours thick sleep down
upon our lids, bringin' on a pain face
for all us kids, bringin' down the stories.
Before lights out, our own leak begins,
and Big Bad Who's in the doorway.

(Very gradual fade-to-black with focus fixed on the
shadow (or ghost) in the doorway. A scratchy version of
Vera Lynn's "We'll Meet Again" plays through the
fade, spanning two centuries of loss and recovery.)

GLOSSARY

(listed in order of first appearance)

(p.11) sky-pilot – a purveyor of flim-flam and spiritual goo.

(p.11) Rougarou – a Cajun lycanthrope.

(p.13) Baba Yaga – female Eastern European / Russian folk character that may serve as a mentor, antagonist, imparter of wisdom or false information. Ambiguity and mutability are common characteristics. She typically lives deep in the woods protected from scrutiny and interference by spells and animal allies. The story of Hansel & Gretel may be derived from the mythology of Baba Yaga.

(p.22) *böser Geist* – (German) bad ghost.

(p.25) *abgefuckt total* – (German slang) completely fucked up.

(p.25) Big Stupid Shoes - elevated platform-like shoes similar to the *buskin* from Greek tragedy, the Roman *cothurnus,* or the 70's UK glam-rock band, *Slade.* These shoes gave the players a literal lift for better visibility and to enhance their stage presence.

(p.31) Spectophilic – a condition of the culture pertaining
to: obsessed by watching, by spectacle. As in "eyes with
gazing fed, caught up in the gaze." Related to
specularity, scopic drive. Derived from concepts of
Herbert Blau, best defined in Blau, Herbert. *to all
appearance: ideology and performance.* Routledge:
New York, NY. 1992.

(p.31) Sefirot – (From the Kabbalah) the emanations, of
which there are ten, through which *Ein Sof* reveals
itself and refreshes and updates all of creation. *Ein Sof*
is the Kabbalistic name for "The Infinite" which exists
before God self-manifests.

(p.42) *Mise-en-scène* – purposeful arrangement of scenic
elements to produce an intended effect; the overall
visual and emotional gestalt of such an arrangement.

(p.43) diegetic eavesdropping – from diegesis or narration.
Mr. Rougarou goes forward into the narrative to listen
and observe – hence the eavesdropping - while making
actual first contact with the Object-Monster.

(p.47) *Wesen* – (German) being. Could also be written as
existenz, but that's considerably more abstract.

(p.51) Goody Rigby and Feathertop – characters in
Nathaniel Hawthorne's short story about power,
hubris, and the essence of human nature, *Feathertop*
(1852).

(p.53) *Jehoshaphat* – originally, a biblically derived call for help in distress (as when Jehoshaphat, a storied king of Judah, cried out to God for help in a battle). No doubt this is conceptually far from aka "Doc Benway's" intention in using the word when coming out of his Spirit-Memory trance. It's just one of the first things that popped into his head.

(p.53) *Vergangenheitsbewältigung* – (German) a post WW2 term from German cultural studies that means, "struggle with the past" with regard to Nazi atrocities committed during the war, most especially the Holocaust. It's obvious aka "Doc Benway" may have quite a few unpleasant things to (dis)remember or justify – though nothing that huge and heinous.

(p.54) Zanni – a stock Commedia dell'arte character that served as both "astute servant" and inveterate trickster.

(p.57) *Zeitschatten* (or *Zeit Schatten*) – time shadow, as in a shadow moving across time. A reversal of the more common *Schatten der Zeit* (shadow of time).

(p.58) pseudobulbar incongruent jag – an emotional incontinence characterized by uncontrollable laughing or crying. This does not mean Miz' Chan actually has a neurological disorder or brain injury, though pseudobulbar behavior is often associated with those kinds of problems. It just looks that way from the outside when each jag starts. After all, she's been through a lot.

(p.61) Gat – old school slang for a hand gun.

(p.65) *insanus terram* – (Latin) "crazy world."

(p.65) Oriflamme – (Middle Ages) battle flag of the King of France based on the banner of the Abbey of St. Denis. Also used to refer to a rallying point or standard during a literal or figurative battle.

(p.65) *Pox Belli* – (Latin-esque) the sickness of war

(p.66) fair dinkum – (Australian slang) vouching for the truth or authenticity of a statement, a person, or an action.

(p.70) *Peregrinatio ad Coeli* – (Latin) leaving home and wandering (Peregrinatio), in this case, toward St. Augustine's concept of Heaven (ad Coeli). Mr. Rougarou probably loads this phrase with deep-seated irony, verging on sarcasm.

(p.76) *absolutio ad cautelam* – (Latin: Roman Catholic Church / Canon Law) literally, "absolution because of doubt." a provisional absolution until all available evidence has been heard and vetted.

(p. 75) *judas-goat* – a goat trained to lead sheep to the killing floor in a slaughterhouse. The sheep are killed while the goat returns to repeat the process with a new group of sheep.

(p.87) Charlotte Corday / *l'ange de l'assassinat* – A Girondist enemy of the Jacobins and their political Reign of Terror in revolutionary France, Corday stabbed to death the prominent Jacobin-Montagnard journalist and political agitator, Jean Paul Marat, while he was bathing in medicinal herbs to treat a chronic skin disease. She was condemned and executed by the Committee for General Security in 1793 by guillotine in the *Place de Greve*, and received the posthumous nickname, *The Angel of Assassination,* from the writer, Alphonse Lamartine, in 1847. The tableau at the top of *Soren K, Just Go Away*, is based on Peter Brook's scene craft for the Peter Weiss play, *The Persecution and Assassination of Jean Paul Marat as Performed by the Inmates of the Asylum of Charenton Under the Direction of the Marquis de Sade* (or, more commonly, *Marat / Sade)*. This scene from the Brooks production is in fact derived from the famous Jacques-Louis David painting (1793), *The Death of Marat.*

(p.94) *Ecce homo* – (Latin - New Testament reference) "behold the man."

(p.95) *Topu, Aos Sí, Duppy, Jumbie, Xapiripe* – magical beings that may be called on for guidance, leverage, assistance, or in other contexts, will resist incursions into their world by beings who don't belong there. *Topu* and *Xapiripe* are Amazonian in origin, while *Duppy* and *Jumbie* are Caribbean, and the *Aos Sí*, Irish. *Jumbies* and *Duppies* are usually malevolent while *Topu* and *Xapiripe* seem more sensitive to motives and intentions. The *Aos Sí* generally disengage from the world of humans but may turn on a dime to obstruct or support.

(p.95) Max Reinhardt's Anarcho-Syndicalist Faeries – at the end of the enchanted sequence in German film director, Max Reinhardt's, 1935 English language version of *A Midsummer Night's Dream* (Warner Brothers), Oberon and his faerie band dissolve into darkness much like the closing of a camera's iris.

(p.110) *Weltanschauung* – (German) A worldview, on which may be based an art, a science, a society, and / or ethical codes of conduct.

(p.110) *Seppuku* – (Japanese) "cutting the belly;" a form of ritual suicide by disembowelment. Seppuku was an integral part of Bushido, the warrior code followed by *samurai* in feudal Japan.

(p.110) Great Leaps Forward, NEP's, Five Year Plans – programmatic attempts by the Soviet policy hierarchy to repair their national economy. The NEP (New Economic Policy which included some small-scale privatization) was Comrade Ulyanov's brainchild. It might have worked but Comrade Ulyanov died *in media res*. Please note: Great Leaps Forward were actually conceived by Mao Zedong and were implemented in China. But the intentions were similar (not identical) and the outcomes, equally catastrophic.

(p.110) *Mise en abyme* – placing a copy of an image inside itself to suggest an infinite recursion of that image, an infinite succession of mirrors effect.

(p.111) Vera Lynn / "We'll Meet Again" – in 1939, the British singer, Vera Lynn recorded "We'll Meet Again," a song that became the foremost nostalgia anthem of WW2. This song was also recorded by Marlene Dietrich and lived through many interpretations on stage and in film, most notably (for me) during the last scene of Stanley Kubrick's *Dr. Strangelove: or How I Learned to Stop Worrying and Love the Bomb* (1964).

About the Author

John Sullivan was an American College Theatre Festival Playwriting Regional finalist, received the 'Jack Kerouac Literary Prize,' 'Writers Voice: New Voices of the West' Award, AZ Arts Fellowships (Poetry & Playwriting), Artists Studio Center Fellowship, WESTAF Fellowship, was a featured playwright at Denver's Changing Scene Summer Play Fest, and an Eco-Arts Performance Fellow from Earth Matters On Stage (University of Oregon). He was Artistic-Producing Director of Theater Degree Zero, collaborated with the Bi-National Theatre Project (Instituto Tecnológico de Nogales, Sonora, Mexico & Cochise College, Douglas AZ) and directed the Augusto Boal / Theatre of the Oppressed focused applied theatre wing at Seattle Public Theater.

For the past fifteen years, he has used Theatre of the Oppressed with vulnerable communities to promote dialogue on toxic exposures-cumulative risk and environmental justice issues with NIEHS environmental health scientists. He was a writer for the online journal, *Community Arts Network / Art in the Public Interest* and has published articles on Community-Based Participatory Research in scientific journals such as *New Solutions, Environmental Health Insights* and *Local Environment.*

His hybrid writing has been published in a variety of print and online journals including: *Hayden's Ferry Review, Black Bear Review, Argy-Bargy, American Writing, California Quarterly, The Lucid Stone, Oddball, OVS,*

Steel Toe Review, Razor: a Literary Magazine, BeZine, Pudding Magazine, Birds Piled Loosely, Madness Muse Press, Harbinger Asylum, Anti-Heroin Chic, Tumblewords: Writers Reading the West, and the *Houston Poetry Festival Anthology.* His chapbook, *Bye-Bye No Fly Zone,* was published in 2019 by Weasel Press (Manvel TX).